HOW TO DEAL

BULLY BUSTERS

LINDEN MCNEILLY

Rourke Educational Media
A Division of Carson Dellosa Education
rourkeeducationalmedia.com

ROURKE'S SCHOOL to HOME CONNECTIONS

BEFORE AND DURING READING ACTIVITIES

Before Reading: *Building Background Knowledge and Vocabulary*

Building background knowledge can help children process new information and build upon what they already know. Before reading a book, it is important to tap into what children already know about the topic. This will help them develop their vocabulary and increase their reading comprehension.

Questions and Activities to Build Background Knowledge:

1. Look at the front cover of the book and read the title. What do you think this book will be about?
2. What do you already know about this topic?
3. Take a book walk and skim the pages. Look at the table of contents, photographs, captions, and bold words. Did these text features give you any information or predictions about what you will read in this book?

Vocabulary: *Vocabulary Is Key to Reading Comprehension*

Use the following directions to prompt a conversation about each word.

- Read the vocabulary words.
- What comes to mind when you see each word?
- What do you think each word means?

Vocabulary Words:

- *anonymous*
- *bigotry*
- *bystanders*
- *consistent*
- *dominate*
- *excluded*
- *harassment*
- *humiliated*
- *peers*
- *status*
- *targets*
- *violation*

During Reading: *Reading for Meaning and Understanding*

To achieve deep comprehension of a book, children are encouraged to use close reading strategies. During reading, it is important to have children stop and make connections. These connections result in deeper analysis and understanding of a book.

Close Reading a Text

During reading, have children stop and talk about the following:

- Any confusing parts
- Any unknown words
- Text to text, text to self, text to world connections
- The main idea in each chapter or heading

Encourage children to use context clues to determine the meaning of any unknown words. These strategies will help children learn to analyze the text more thoroughly as they read.

When you are finished reading this book, turn to page 46 for **Text-Dependent Questions** and an **Extension Activity**.

TABLE OF CONTENTS

CHAPTER 1

WHAT IS BULLYING?

Alex is a popular boy who plays rough. When Robert gets on the bus, he dreads walking by Alex. Alex always pulls him down in the seat beside him. Alex wants to wrestle, but he is much stronger than Robert. Alex puts Robert in a headlock and pulls Robert's arm behind his back, pretending to show him new wrestling moves. Robert says, "Ow! Stop!" Alex just says, "Aw, come on. Fight like a man." That makes everyone around them laugh. Robert wants to get away, and he has to fight back tears. He feels **humiliated**.

He's a big *bully*. She's really a *frenemy*. You've heard these terms, but what do they really mean? How can you recognize bullies when they sometimes act like friends? What can you do if you are bullied, or if someone else is?

Bullying is a specific kind of mean treatment. It is repeated, done on purpose, and meant to cause harm. Usually the bully has more power than the victim, either through strength, age, or **status**. Bullies can use physical force, words, sexual actions, **bigotry**, the internet, or the power of popularity to control others and show power.

Bullying or Just Bad Manners?

People sometimes confuse bullying with rudeness or meanness. Rudeness, such as stepping in front of someone in line, is not bullying unless it's done more than once. Meanness, such as yelling at a teammate for a mistake, is not bullying either, unless it continues or worsens.

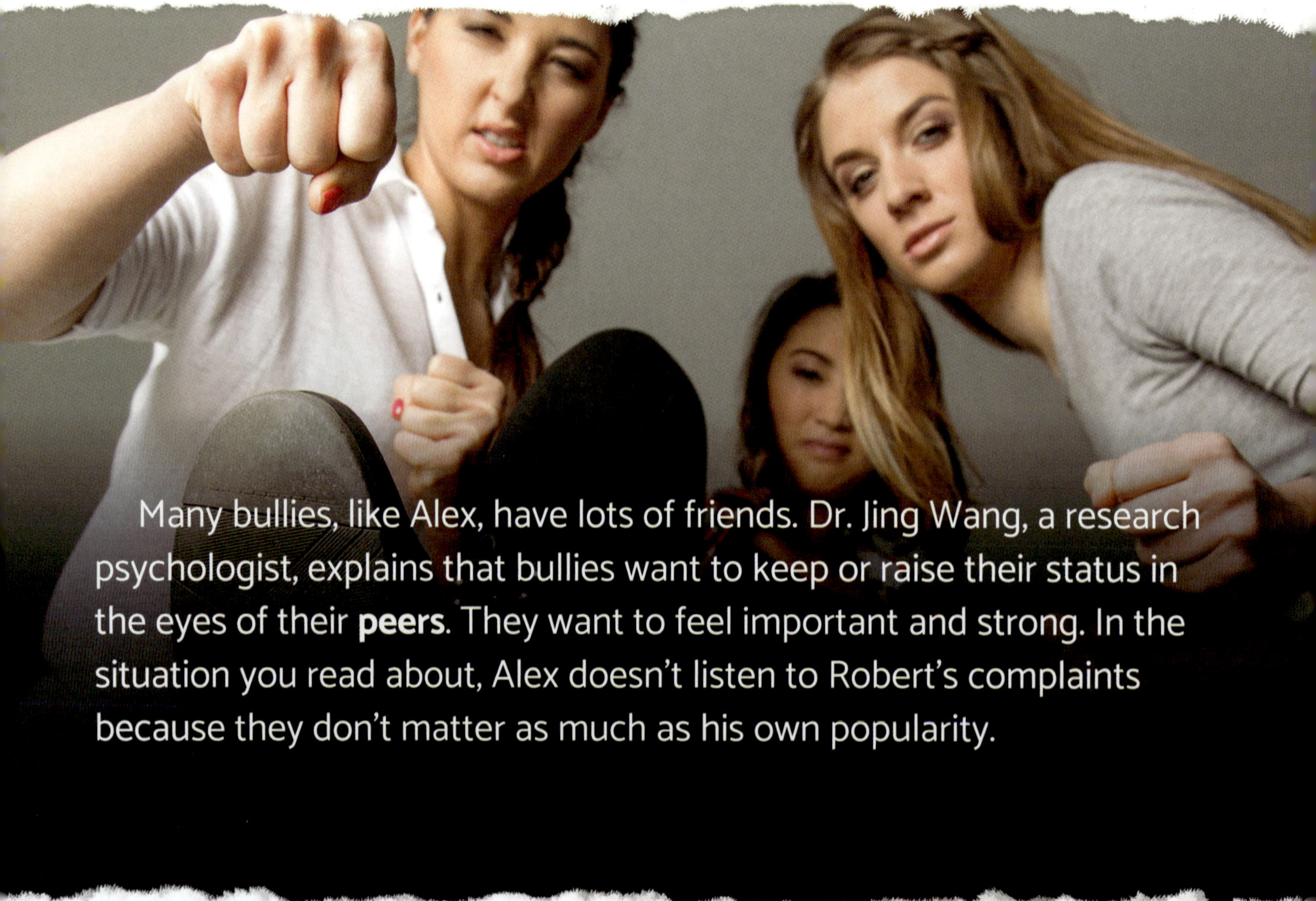

Many bullies, like Alex, have lots of friends. Dr. Jing Wang, a research psychologist, explains that bullies want to keep or raise their status in the eyes of their **peers**. They want to feel important and strong. In the situation you read about, Alex doesn't listen to Robert's complaints because they don't matter as much as his own popularity.

Tattling or Telling?

One of the biggest reasons bullies get away with hurting others is because kids don't want to tell adults. Some adults even discourage "tattling." The difference between tattling and telling is that tattling is meant to get someone in trouble. Telling is meant to stop someone from hurting another person–including yourself.

A bully like Alex might have a family member who treats him or her the same way. Bullies sometimes learn to get attention from others by being rough. Because they are bullied in their private lives, they act out their frustration and anger on victims of their own.

In situations like these, you should recognize that someone behaving like Alex is not a good friend. Though it's difficult, you must stand up for yourself. You should firmly and clearly tell the bully to stop. You should also avoid any physical contact with the person.

In the story you read, what should Robert do? One solution would be for him to find another bus seat away from Alex and to sit with people who will support him. To prevent Alex from bullying others, Robert should tell a trusted adult about how Alex treats him.

CHAPTER 2

PREJUDICE IS NO JOKE

Fadia, Benjamin, and Yesenia are in the same table group in class. Fadia is Muslim and wears a head scarf, or hijab. Benjamin tugs on Fadia's hijab. This is a big **violation** of space for Fadia, but she feels self-conscious making a fuss. She tries to move her chair away from Benjamin, but he just comes closer. Benjamin jokes around a lot. He asks Fadia, "Were your relatives 9/11 pilots?" This horrifies Fadia, but she is too upset to respond. Though Yesenia hears, she doesn't do anything to stop Benjamin, and never says anything to Fadia. Fadia feels unsafe and alone.

Jokers like Benjamin use prejudicial bullying disguised as humor. They target people for their religion, race, skin color, sexual identity, or gender. Referring to 9/11 is Benjamin's way of falsely blaming Fadia's culture for those attacks. This is bigotry.

Prejudicial bullying can open the door to hate crimes. **Bystanders** like Yesenia are part of the problem if they don't call out the bullying. Bystanders can be held accountable for hate crimes if they do not try to stop them.

Bystanders Hold the Power

Bystander approval is important to bullies. This means bystanders have the power to stop bullying, says counselor Signe Whitson. So why don't bystanders speak up? Often, they are afraid of becoming victims themselves, or they are torn between two friends. They want to be included, even when it means going along with being cruel.

Everyone has a right to a safe classroom environment. If you are bullied at school because of who you are, you should calmly and forcefully tell the bully to stop bothering you. Point out in front of others that the things the bully is saying show prejudice, racism, or cruelty, even if you are shy or nervous.

In the situation you read about, Fadia should look for help from others. She should ask Yesenia to help by calling out Benjamin's racism. She should ask other students to get involved by telling Benjamin to knock it off. She and others should report the behavior to school authorities.

Snappy Comebacks to Bullying

Offering a friendly smile to show the victim you care is a good first step to helping build safety against bullying. Then, go beyond a smile and defend victims by standing up to bullies. Use phrases like the ones below. Practice them at home first.

- *Hey, that's racist.*
- *Stop it!*
- *You're totally out of line.*
- *Knock it off and leave her alone!*

CHAPTER 3

FRIEND OR FRENEMY?

Kiki is the most popular girl in Sasha's grade at school. She's often very friendly, and lots of people like her. At lunch, Kiki tells everyone where to sit, sometimes inviting Sasha to sit close to her. "I like your sweater," Kiki might tell Sasha before talking to her all through lunch. But during gym one day, Kiki gathered some of the girls to hang out with her. When Sasha started to join them, Kiki shook her head and turned away. The other girls laughed as Kiki **excluded** Sasha from the group. Sasha had no idea what she'd done wrong.

Kiki is a relational bully, or *frenemy*. Sometimes, frenemies can be nice. They use the promise of friendship and popularity to control others. Since they have lots of followers, they can get away with telling others what to do. They love social power.

A relational bully can exclude anyone, and it can happen at any moment. No one but the bully knows the rules of the cruel game. Because they fear being left out themselves, the bully's close circle of friends goes along with the meanness. This only reinforces the bully's popularity.

Who's Popular?

Think about someone who is popular at your school. Is that person actually liked and admired, or feared? Does he or she spread friendliness and include others, or make rules about who is in and who is out? You can stop making bullies popular by calling out mean behavior and not following frenemies.

In the story you read, Sasha has to realize that Kiki is a frenemy, not a friend. It is not Sasha's fault or the result of anything she did. When someone near you turns friendship on and off to control you, it's important to recognize that and not buy into it.

If you have this kind of relationship with someone, you should distance yourself and find friends who are safe, kind, and **consistent**. When you see a frenemy bullying others, you can say things like, "That's not cool," or "I can't believe you did that."

Girls Can Bully Differently Than Boys

Girls use relational bullying more than boys, who use physical bullying more. Relational bullying creates isolation, making the victim feel damaged and unwanted. If you are experiencing relational bullying, look outside the popular group for support. Often, others experience it too. Sometimes those people make better friends.

CHAPTER

4

IT'S ALL IN THE WAY YOU SAY IT

Dario and Haven are in the same science class. Dario is young for his grade. He is very shy and rarely speaks up in class because he sometimes stutters. When the teacher calls on him, it takes a lot of effort for Dario to speak aloud. Haven whispers things like, “Here we go again, Dario the d-d-d-dork” and “He’s so stu-stu-stu-stupid.” Other students laugh, which makes Haven do it even more. The teacher doesn’t hear it. Dario hates going to class and feels sick when he is bullied. He wants to skip school or get switched to another science class.

Haven is a verbal bully. This type of bully repeatedly uses words to make others feel bad, ashamed, or embarrassed. Despite the famous saying about sticks and stones, words can and do hurt, especially when others laugh at them. Verbal bullying can cause school avoidance, depression, and more.

More Snappy Comebacks

You can stand up to bullies. Use comebacks like the ones below. Practice them at home in front of a mirror, keeping a normal tone of voice. You will be ready if bullying happens to you or someone around you.

Bullies sometimes choose **targets** based on the way they look or act. They find what they consider to be a weakness and make fun of it. In the situation you read about, Haven targets Dario because of his shyness and stuttering. This type of bullying feels very personal and therefore very painful.

Victims of verbal bullying often feel alone. But reaching out to others is essential. If you are the victim of verbal bullying at school, you must tell your teacher and ask for a seat or class change. If the teacher doesn't take action, you should go to other school authorities.

Asking others to help has been shown to shut bullying down. Nearby students can say, “That’s rude!” or “Shush, I can’t hear the teacher.” They can also vow to stop laughing at the bully’s remarks, taking away his or her power to “entertain.”

Verbal Bullying: Sneak Attack

Verbal bullying is hard to catch because it’s done quietly, often away from adults. If you see or hear bullying, you should tell the adult in charge. Ask him or her to walk around more to see what is happening, or to move the bully away so the meanness will stop.

CHAPTER 5

BULLYING IN CYBERSPACE

Last summer, Lily, Elaine, and Palma were best friends. They spent lots of time at the beach, sunning, swimming, and taking funny photos of each other. This year, Palma has made some new friends, so she isn't hanging out with Lily or Elaine very much. Palma's new friends told her there is a fake social media account with her name on it that features lots of bikini photos. **Anonymous** people have made rude comments about Palma's body and suggested she's trying to get attention. Palma confronted Lily and Elaine, but they just pretended they didn't know what she was talking about.

Lily and Elaine are cyberbullies. Cyberbullying is a special kind of bullying done mostly online. It's often hard to link to one person. It uses the rapid spreading and sharing of fake or embarrassing information and photos to cause harm.

The fast pace of cyberbullying is part of what makes it so damaging and so hard to control. But the worst thing about it, according to Robin Kowalski, a professor of psychology at Clemson University, is how people feel free to be cruel when they don't have to sign their real names.

The Internet: Forever Yours

One of the most important facts to know about the internet is that information on it never really goes away. Once something is posted, it can always be found again. So it's essential to make good choices about photos others take of you. Control your image and reputation by thinking ahead. Before you post or share photos, think about the effect it could have.

If you are the victim of cyberbullying, take screen shots of the evidence and ask an adult to help shut down the site immediately. You should question the suspected bullies and insist that all original photos be permanently removed from their phones and online accounts.

Cyberbullying can make you feel like everyone is against you. It's a good idea to take a break from social media or at least to change your account settings so you can block people as needed. You should also try hard to not take any of the comments seriously or personally.

Super Sad? There's Help

Sometimes, you might feel alone and think that everyone is against you. You might experience low moods, which can lead to thoughts of self-harm or suicide. Always tell someone if you feel like harming yourself. Tell a trusted adult such as a parent, relative, teacher, clergy member, or medical professional who can help you get the support you need. The National Suicide Prevention Lifeline is available 24 hours a day to provide help at 1-800-273-8255.

CHAPTER 6

TOO CLOSE FOR COMFORT

The teacher made Brady and Mei partners in language arts class. They are required to work together, which Mei hates. Brady says, "Ooh, that sweater really fits your body. You're so sexy." He sits too close, makes kissing noises in her ear, and "accidentally" touches her chest while passing a book. She says, "Stop it! That's not funny!" But Brady just laughs it off, telling her, "Don't take it so seriously! You're cute when you're mad." Then he aims his phone at her (without her permission), saying, "I need a photo of my girlfriend."

Brady is using sexual bullying to **dominate** and control Mei. This kind of bullying can happen between any two or more people as long as it has a sexual quality, is repeated, and is unwanted by the receiver. The bully wants to feel power over the victim.

No matter what your gender or sexual orientation is, if you are receiving repeated and uninvited touching, suggestions, name-calling, crude comments, or vulgar gestures, you are being sexually bullied. Girls sometimes engage in sexual bullying by calling other girls names or by making rude comments about their bodies. Boys can be sexual bullies when they tease other boys about how they look or who they like.

It's Not Because He Likes You

Our culture sometimes calls for girls to treat unwanted attention as a compliment. Some people even suggest that when a boy bullies, it's because he "likes" the girl. But sexual bullying is about power, not flirting or attraction. Sexual bullies feel entitled to do whatever they want. They can become perpetrators of sexual assault.

Victims of sexual bullying need to take quick action. The first step is to call out the bully firmly and strongly. Repeat if necessary, despite the bully's insistence that it's all in fun. Victims should enlist others to pressure the bully to stop the **harassment**.

The next step is to tell a trusted adult. Know that you absolutely deserve a safe, bully-free environment. If nothing improves, seek out another authority. Stick up for yourself. Ask firmly for a seating change at school or on the bus, a change in class assignment, more adult supervision in a certain area, or whatever will make you feel safe.

Bullying has many faces. Often, a situation may involve several types of bullying at once. Whatever form bullying takes, it's always wrong, and it's never the victim's fault.

Bullying can lead to strong feelings of isolation, sadness, and hopelessness. But there is hope. If you are bullied, remember that you deserve respect and safety. When you find the courage to call out bullies, you can change your own life. If you are a bystander, you command a lot of power when you identify bullies and stand up to them. It's up to each one of us to be a bully buster.

ACTIVITY

SHIELD OF POWER

Never forget that you control many things in your life. There is always something you can do to improve a bad situation. This activity will arm you with a plan of action to battle bullies and protect yourself and others.

Draw a large shield in the center of a sheet of paper. Draw five large jewel shapes or other shapes on the shield. Leave space inside each shape for writing. Decorate the rest of the shield with pictures and words that tell what makes you special and why you deserve respect.

In the area outside the shield, around the margins of the paper, write things that you can't control about bullying. Include encountering bullies, reasons why people bully, where bullying might happen, peers being bullied, how bystanders react, or other ideas.

Inside each jewel shape, write one thing you CAN control about bullying. Include not being a bully yourself, not being a quiet bystander, not laughing at bullies, calling bullies out, telling trusted adults, or other ideas.

GLOSSARY

anonymous (uh-NAH-nuh-muhs): written, done, or given by a person whose name is not known or made public

bigotry (BIG-uh-tree): holding strong opinions and prejudices, especially those that are intolerant toward people of other races, nationalities, and religions

bystanders (BYE-stan-durz): people who are at a place where something happens to someone else; spectators

consistent (kuhn-SIS-tuhnt): always behaving in the same way or according to the same principles; predictable

dominate (DAH-muh-nate): to control or to rule

excluded (ik-SKLOOD-id): kept from joining or taking part in something

harassment (huh-RAS-mint): the act of bothering or annoying someone again and again

humiliated (hyoo-MIL-ee-ate-tid): made to feel foolish or embarrassed

peers (peerz): equals, or people of the same age, rank, or standing

status (STA-tuhs): a person's rank or position in a group, an organization, or a society

targets (TAHR-gits): people who are criticized or made fun of

violation (vye-uh-LAY-shuhn): the act of disturbing or harming rudely

INDEX

TEXT-DEPENDENT QUESTIONS

1. What is relational bullying?
2. What is the role of the bystander in bullying?
3. Why are most adults unaware of verbal bullying?
4. How does our culture make it hard for girls to recognize sexual bullying?
5. Why is cyberbullying so much harder to deal with than most other kinds of bullying?

EXTENSION ACTIVITY

Think of times you have witnessed or been the victim of bullying. Choose one and write it like the scenarios featured in this book. Include the outcome. Then, come up with three things the victim and the bystanders could have done differently. Rewrite the scenario with those actions in it along with a possible new ending.

BIBLIOGRAPHY

Coloroso, Barbara. *The Bully, the Bullied, and the Not-So-Innocent Bystander.* New York: William Morrow, 2016.

Kowalski, Robin M., and Susan P. Limber. "Electronic Bullying Among Middle School Students." *Journal of Adolescent Health* 41, no. 6 (December 2007): S22–S30.

Miller, Cindy, and Cynthia Lowen. *The Essential Guide to Bullying: Prevention and Intervention.* New York: Alpha Books, 2012.

Olweus, Dan. *Bullying at School: What We Know and What We Can Do.* Hoboken, NJ: Wiley-Blackwell, 1993.

Pickhardt, Carl. *Why Good Kids Act Cruel.* Naperville, IL: Sourcebooks, 2010.

Rivkin, Jennifer. *Physical Bullying.* New York: Crabtree Publishing Company, 2013.

Wang, Jing, et al. "School Bullying Among Adolescents in the United States: Physical, Verbal, Relational, and Cyber." *Journal of Adolescent Health* 45, no. 4 (October 2009): 368–375.

Whitson, Signe. *8 Keys to End Bullying.* New York: W. W. Norton & Company, 2014.

ABOUT THE AUTHOR

Linden McNeilly has written numerous books for young readers. She taught school for many years and now spends her time researching crazy facts about insects, flowers, and history, painting birds, and enjoying the outdoors with her family on the Central Coast of California.

www.rourkeeducationalmedia.com

PHOTO CREDITS: Cover photos: (Top) Rawpixel.com / Shutterstock.com, (Bottom) SpeedKingz / Shutterstock.com; Page 4-5: Lisa Mckown | Dreamstime.com; Page 6-7: istock.com | monkeybusinessimages, istock.com | Highwaystarz-Photography, istock.com | Catalin205.; Page 8-9: istock.com | vizualni, shutterstock.com | Africa Studio, 462953453 istock.com | ackF.; Page 10-11: 88725679 ©Lisa Mckown | Dreamstime.com, shutterstock.com | Rawpixel.com, istock.com | Daisy-Daisy.; Page 12-13: istock.com | Ridofranz.; Page 14-15: 36777501 ©Tyler Olson | Dreamstime.com, 129528654 ©Lightfieldstudiosprod | Dreamstime.com.; Page 16-17: istock.com | DGLimages, istock.com | Professor25, istock.com | DGLimages.; Page 18-19: shutterstock.com | Monkey Business Images; Page 20-21: shutterstock.com | Monkey Business Images, istock.com | Zinkevych; Page 22-23: shutterstock.com | Dusan Petkovic, shutterstock.com | LightField Studios; Page 24-25: istock.com | monkeybusinessimages; Page 26-27: shutterstock.com | Sasa Prudkov, shutterstock.com | Syda Productions; Page 28-29: shutterstock.com | Syda Productions, istock.com | edwardmallia, istock.com | shironosov; Page 30-31: istock.com | fotojog; Page 32-33: istock.com | AndreyPopov, istock.com | AntonioGuillem; Page 34-35: istock.com | LeszekCzerwonka, istock.com | AntonioGuillem; Page 36-37: shutterstock.com | Sergey Furtaev; Page 38-39: Tero Vesalainen | Dreamstime.com, kali9 | istock.com, Daisy Daisy | Shutterstock.com; Page 40-41: shutterstock.com | Luis Molinero, istock.com | monkeybusinessimages; Page 42-43: shutterstock.com | RimDream, istock.com | omgimages.

Edited by: Kim Thompson

Produced by Blue Door Education for Rourke Educational Media. Cover and interior design by: Jennifer Dydyk

Library of Congress PCN Data

Bully Busters / Linden McNeilly
(How To Deal)
ISBN 978-1-73161-490-2 (hard cover)
ISBN 978-1-73161-297-7 (soft cover)
ISBN 978-1-73161-595-4 (e-Book)
ISBN 978-1-73161-700-2 (e-Pub)
Library of Congress Control Number: 2019932375

Rourke Educational Media
Printed in the United States of America,
North Mankato, Minnesota